By Author: Beatrice Harrison
Book Title: Steampunk Superheroes and Villains: An Adult Coloring Book Features Over 30 Pages Giant Super Jumbo Large Designs of Superheroes, Warriors, and Goddesses for Relaxation

Adults enjoy coloring awesome steampunk superheroes, warriors, and goddess for stress relief, relaxation, and fun

Biography

Beatrice Harrison enjoys creating books, traveling, exercising, church

LICENSED IMAGES! No part of this book may be reproduced

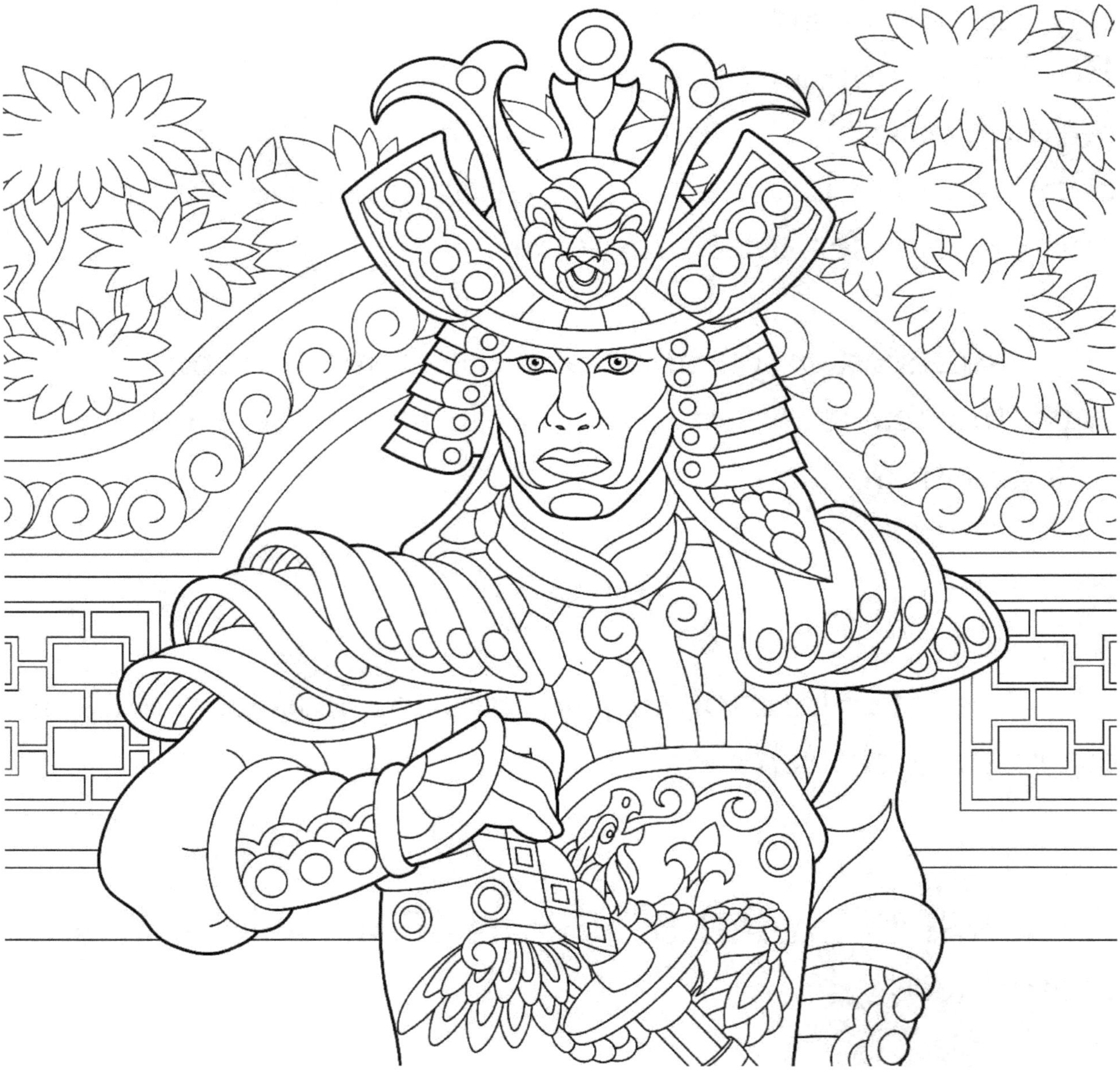

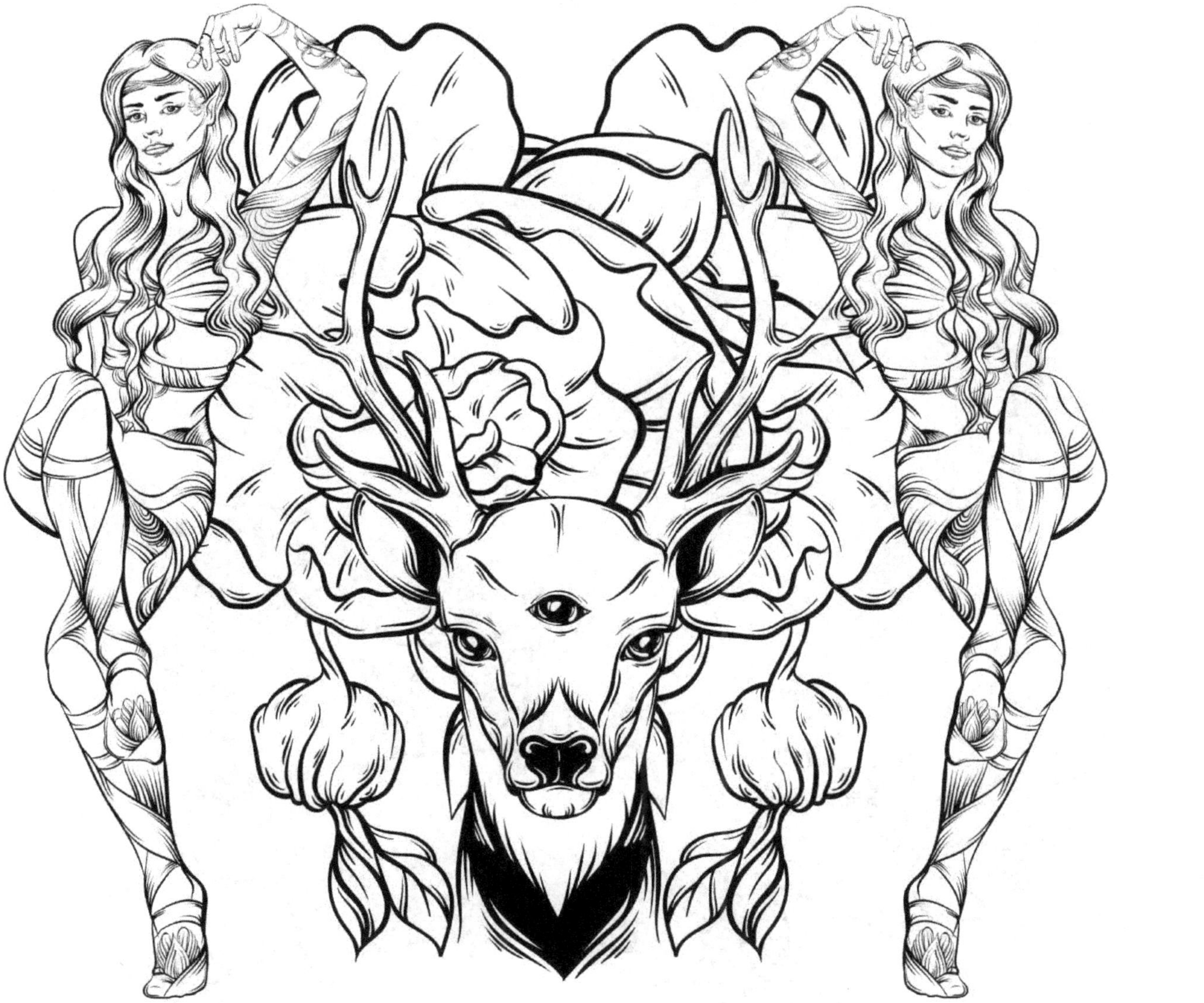

Gemini

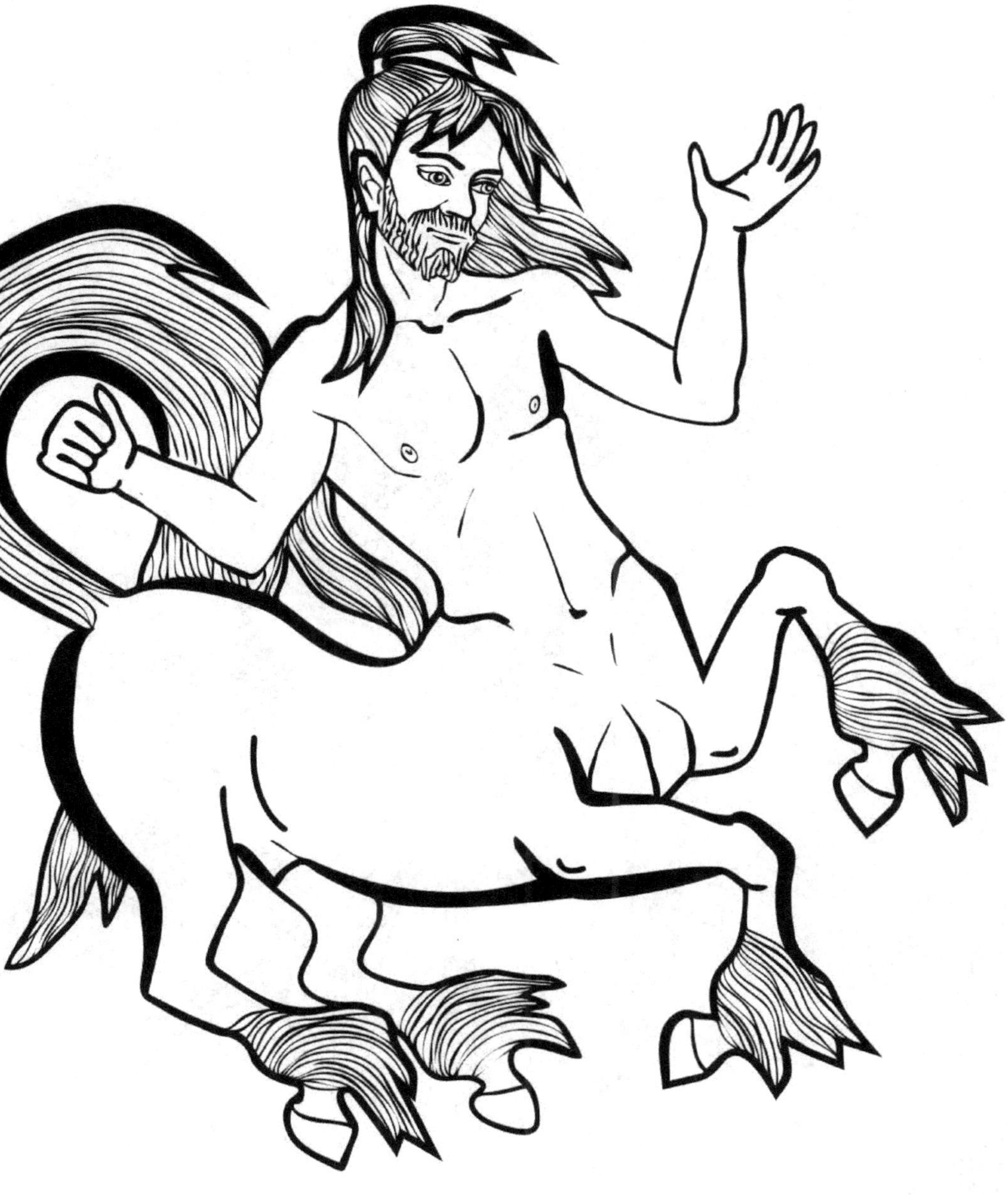

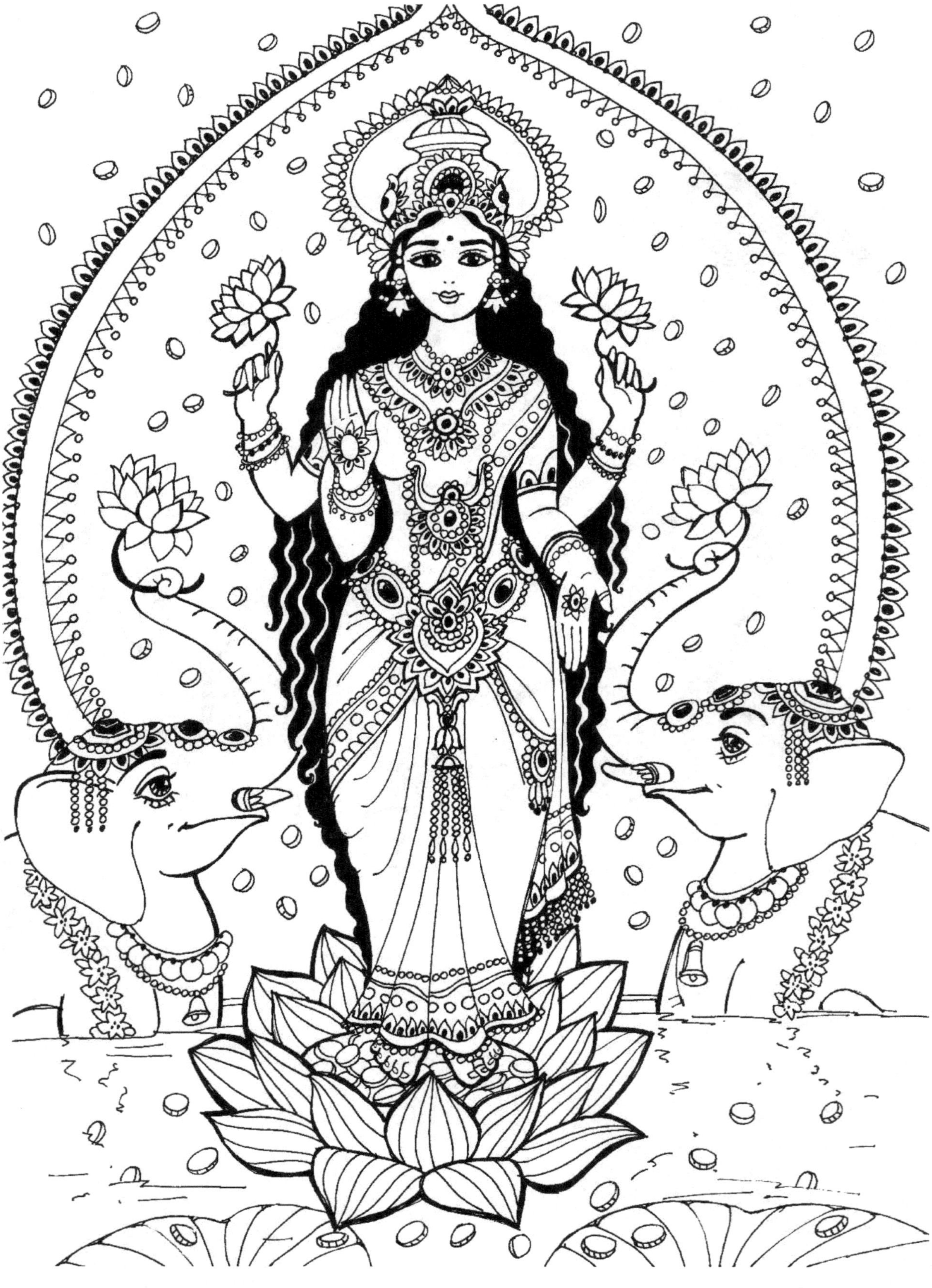

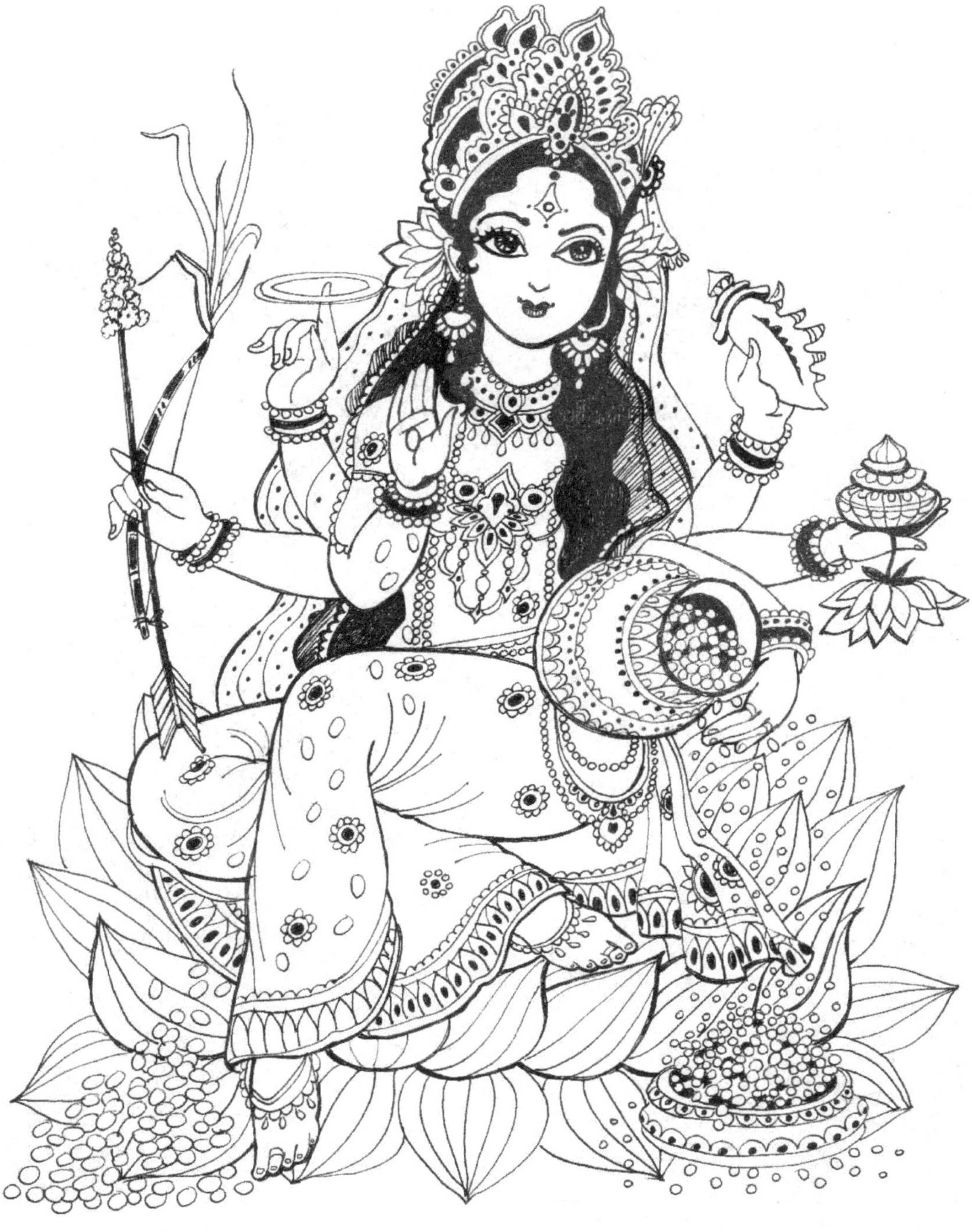

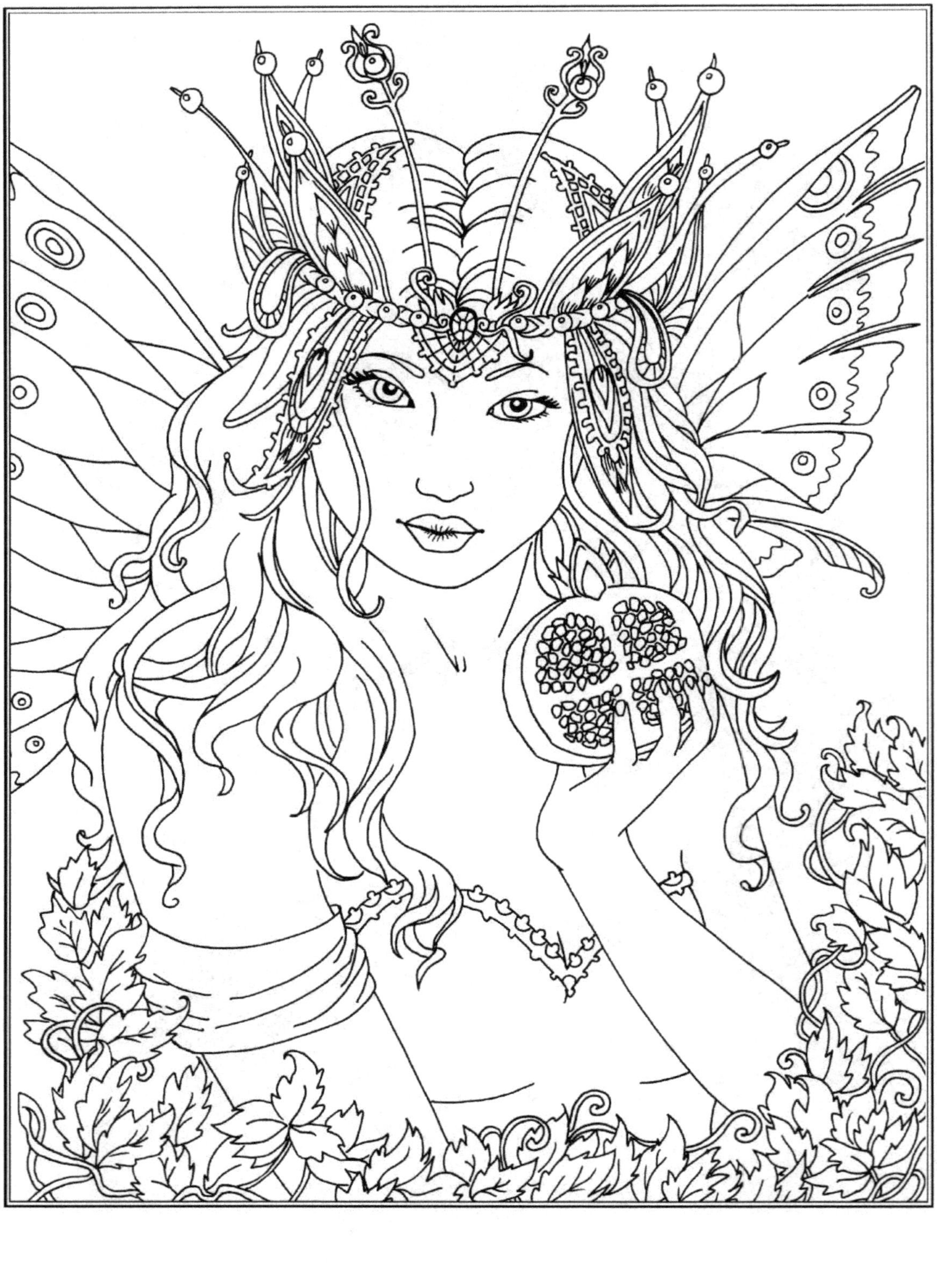

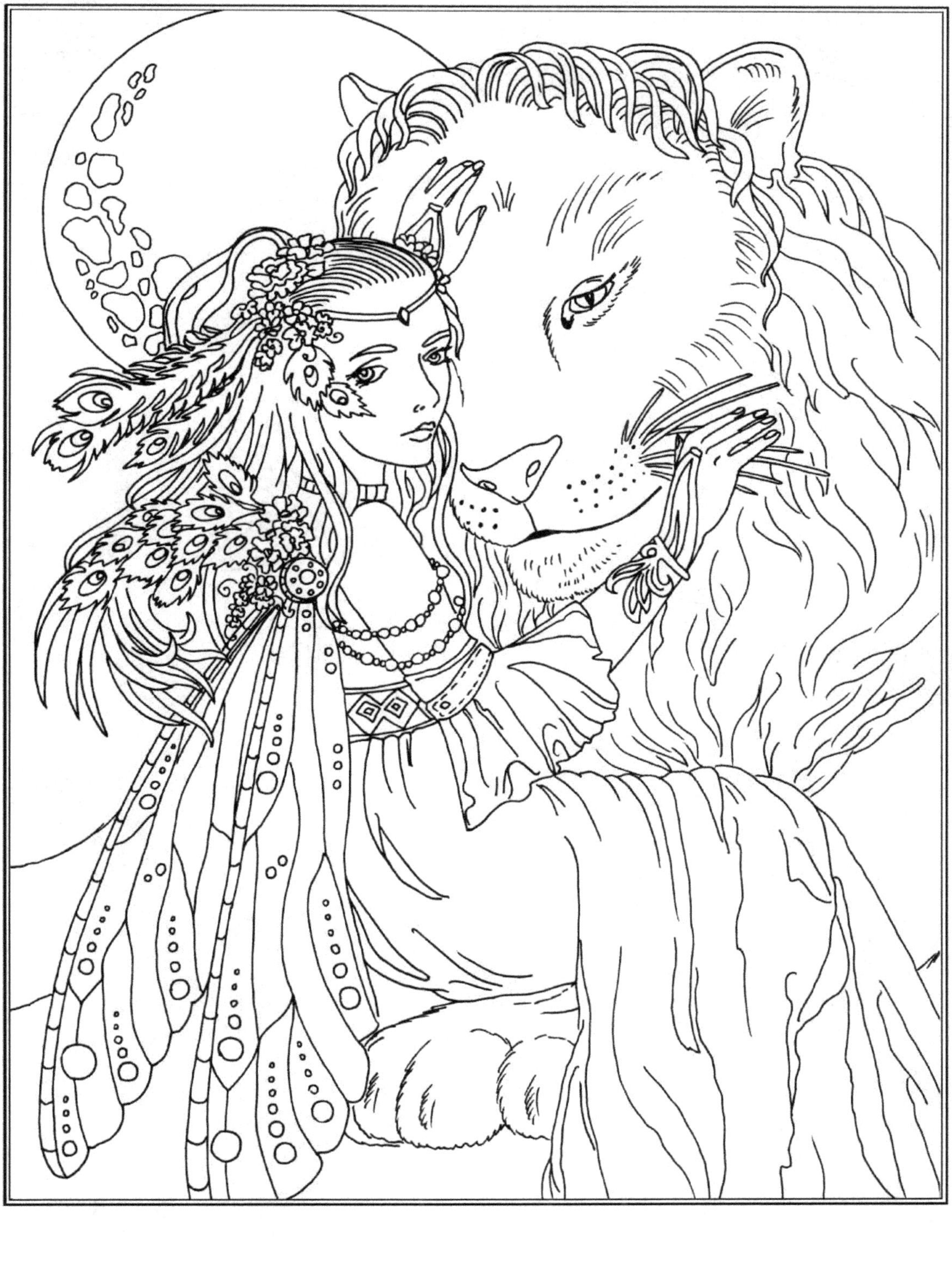

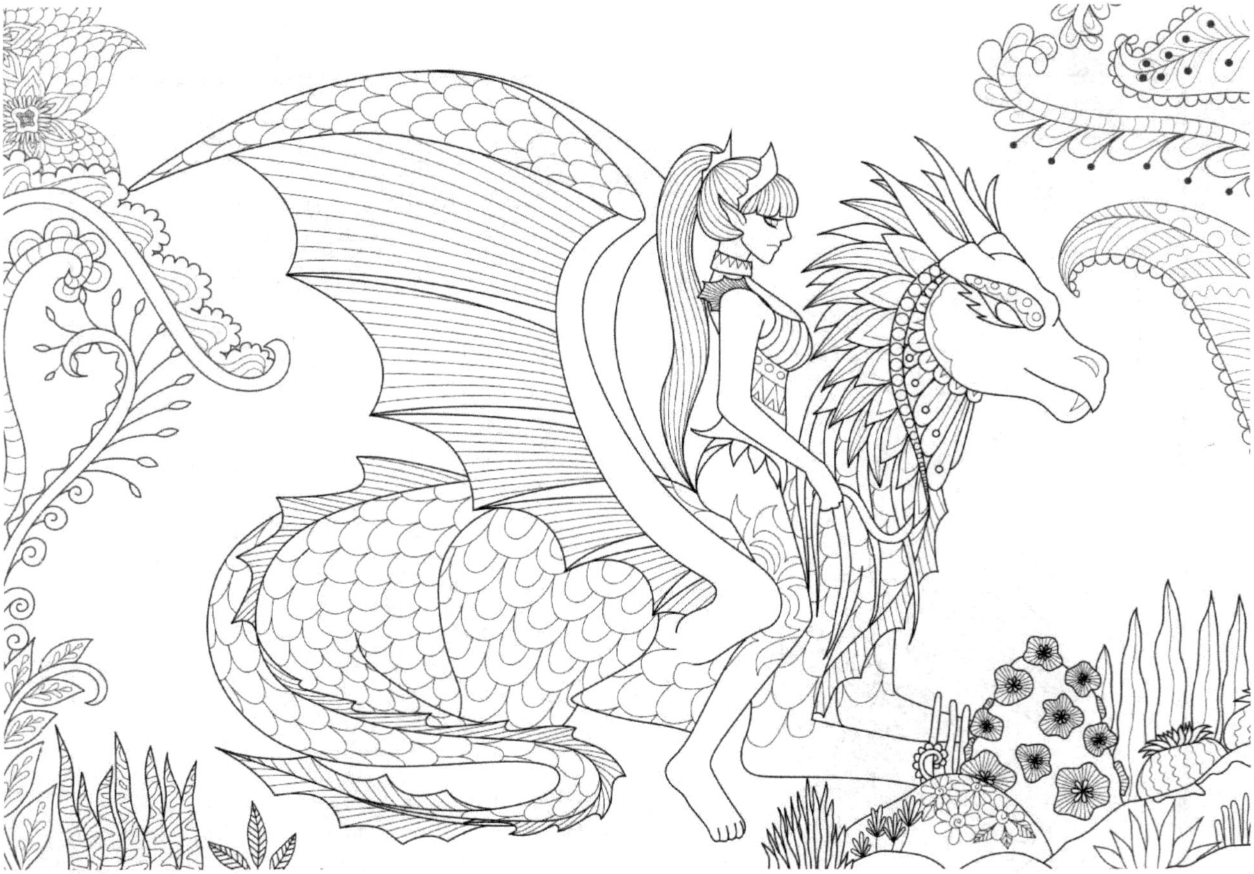

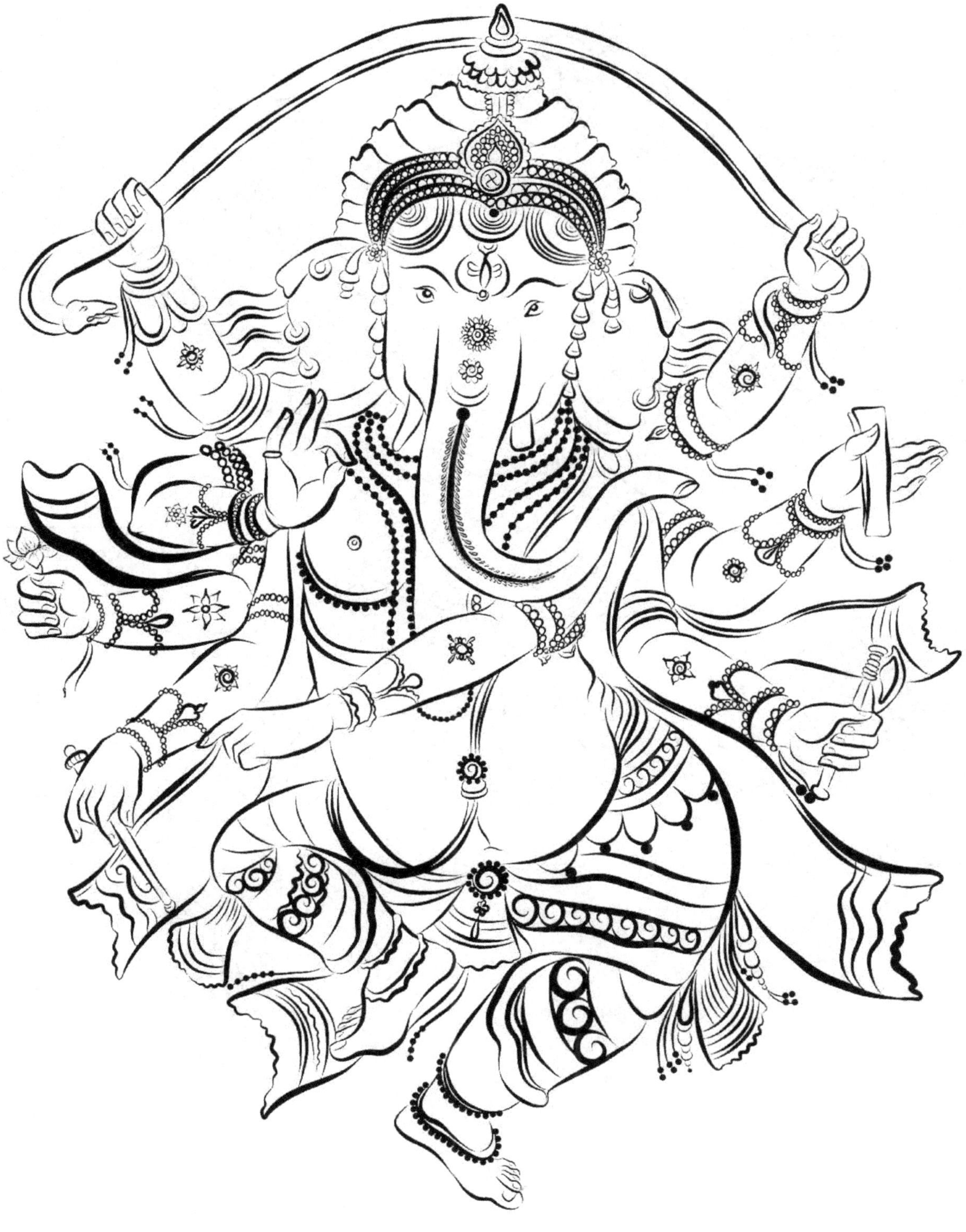

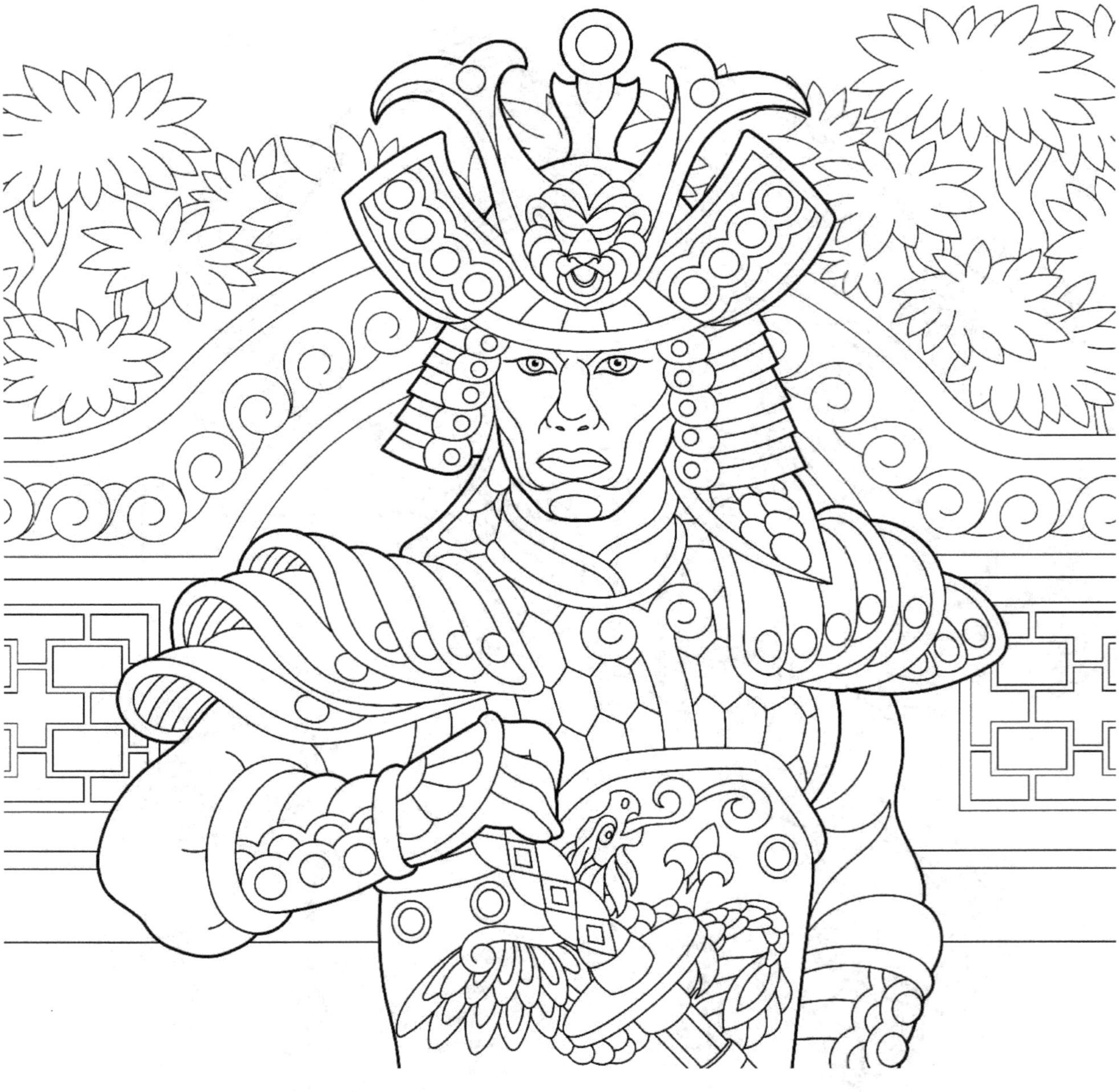

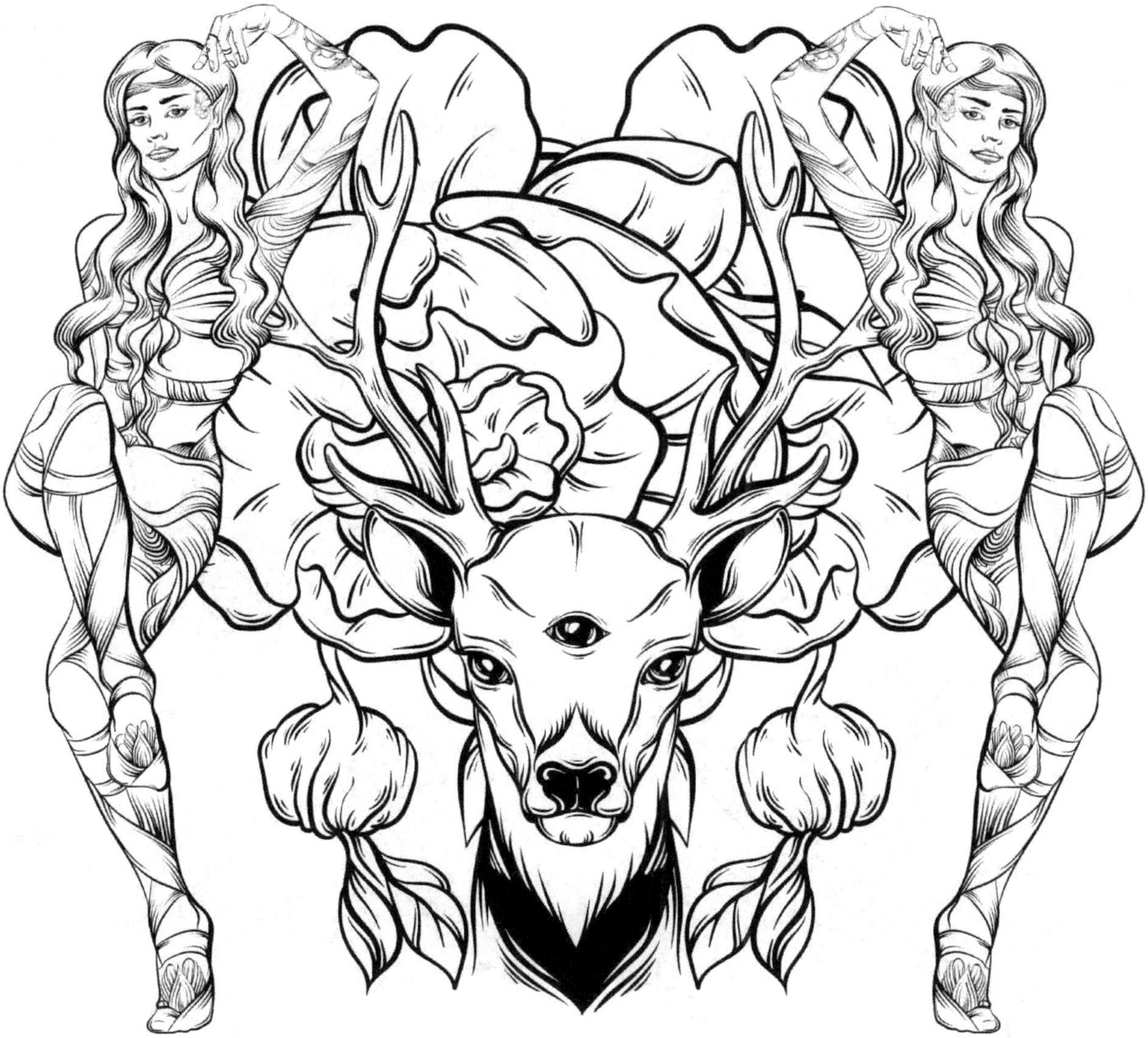

Gemini

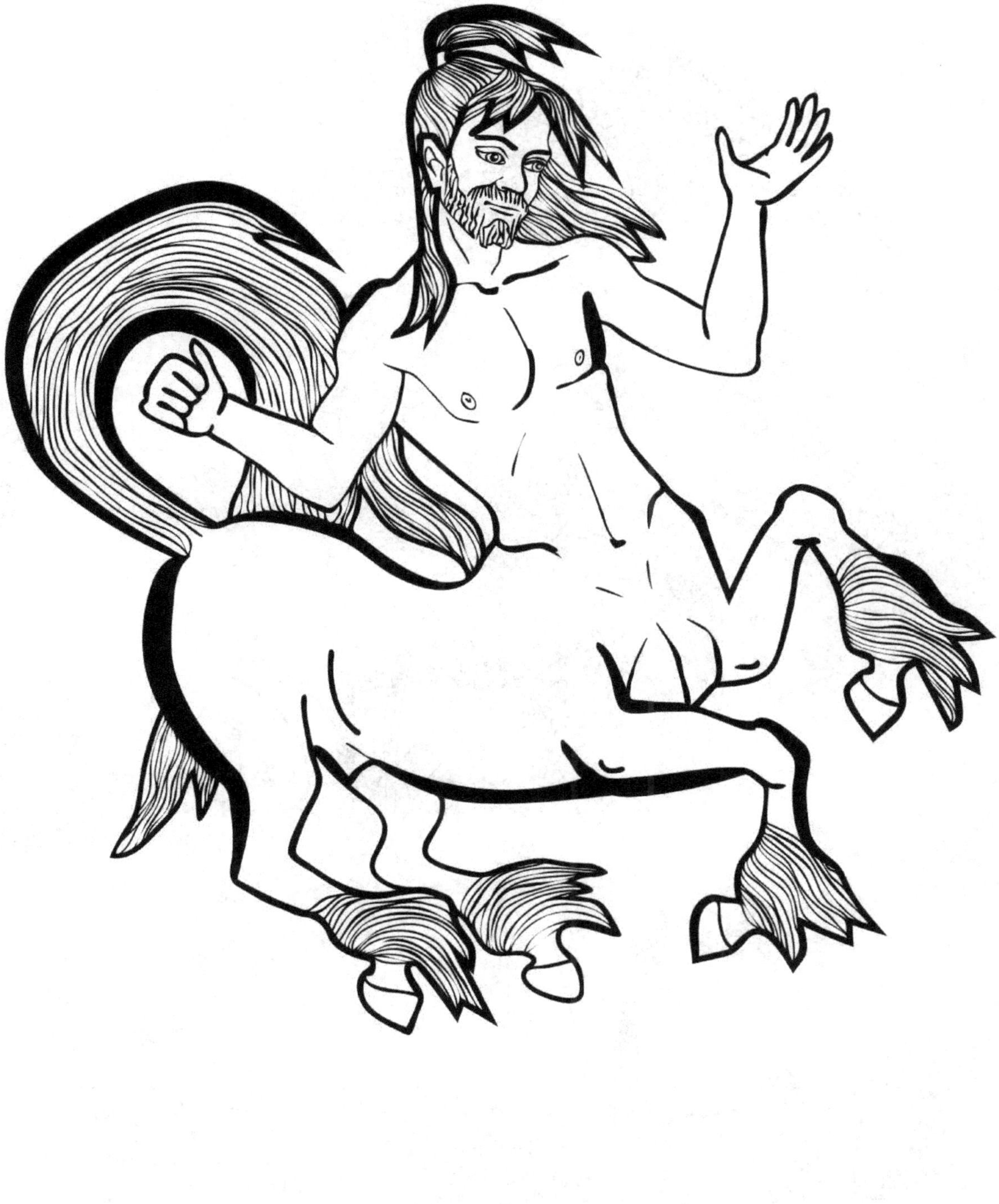

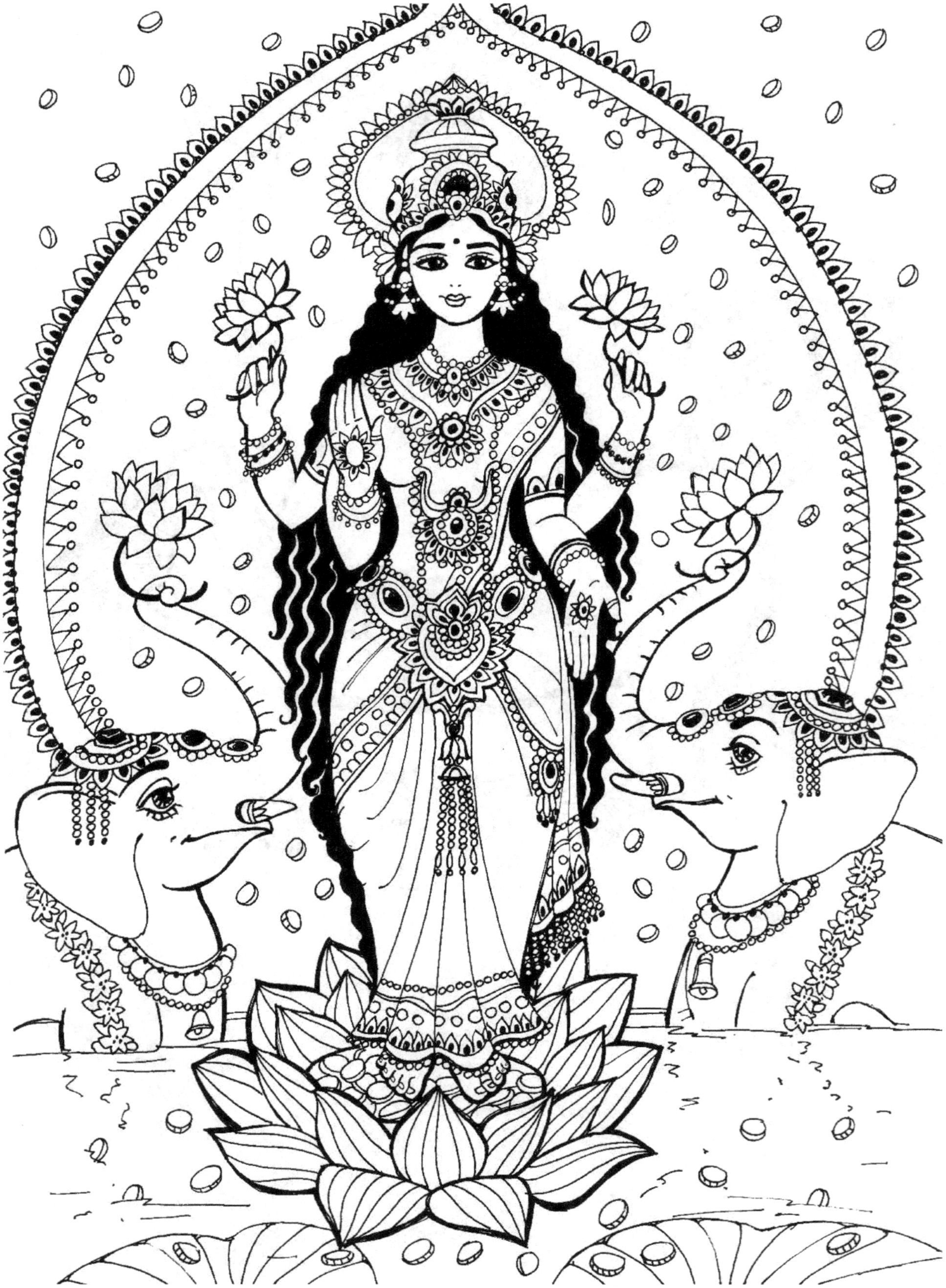

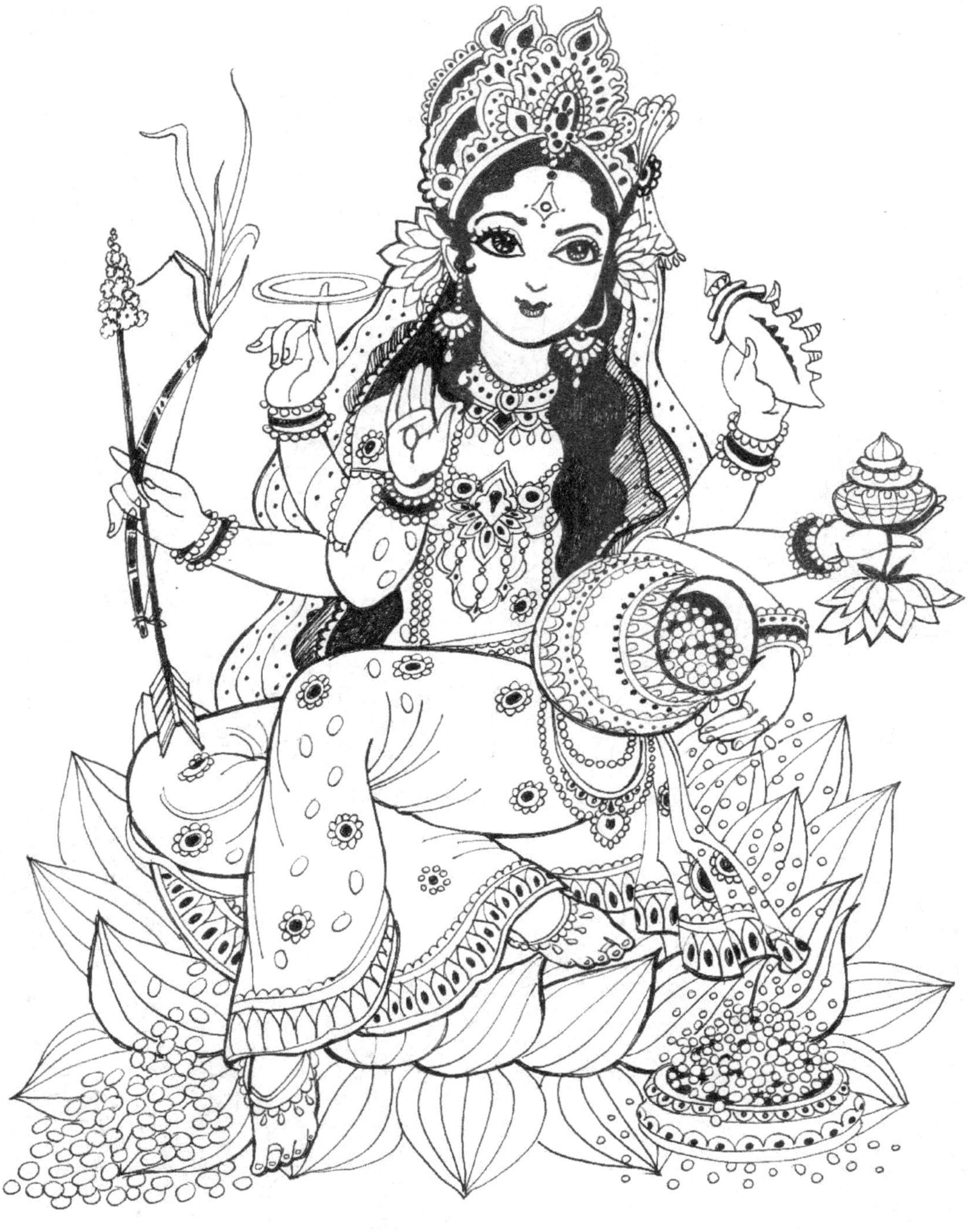

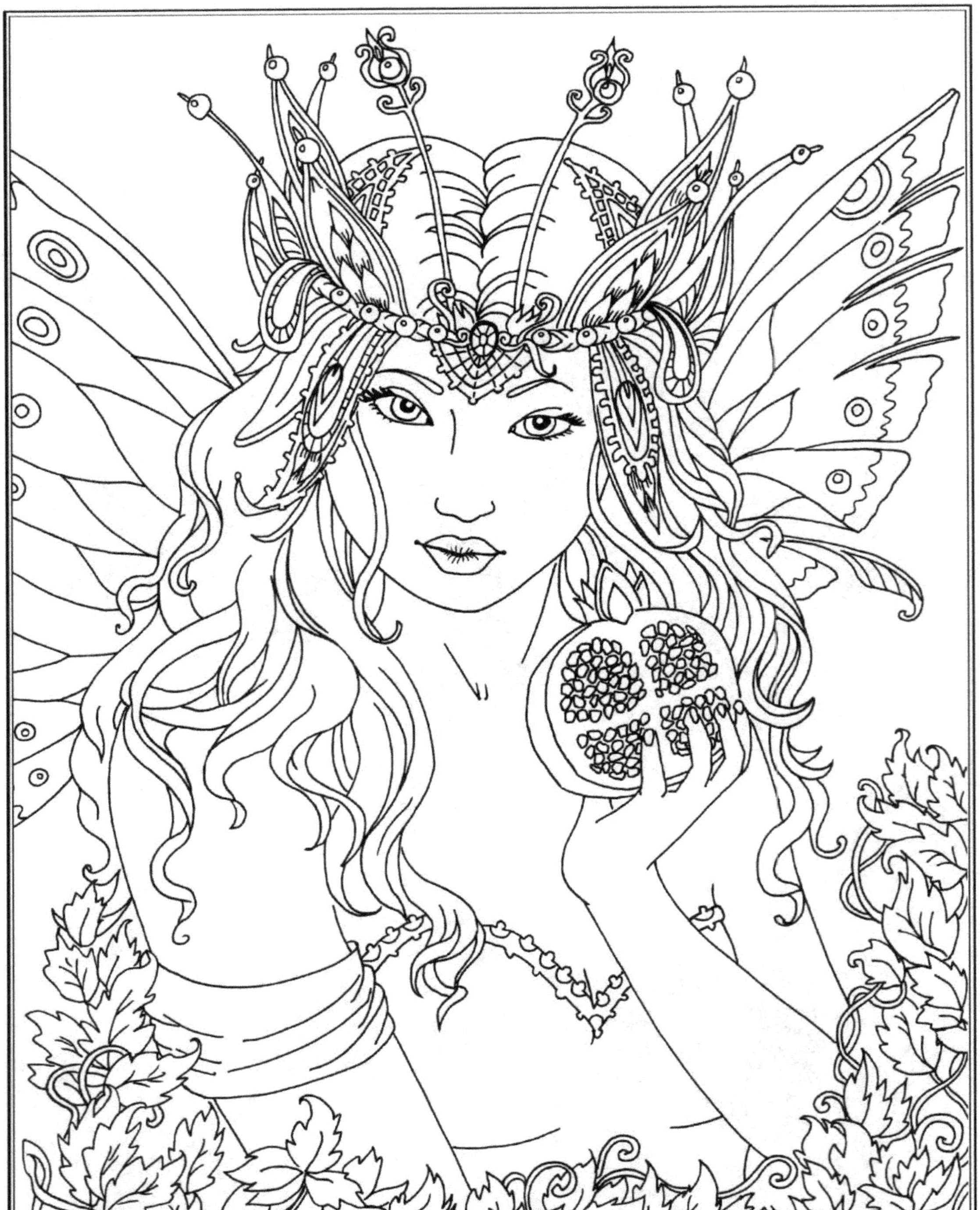

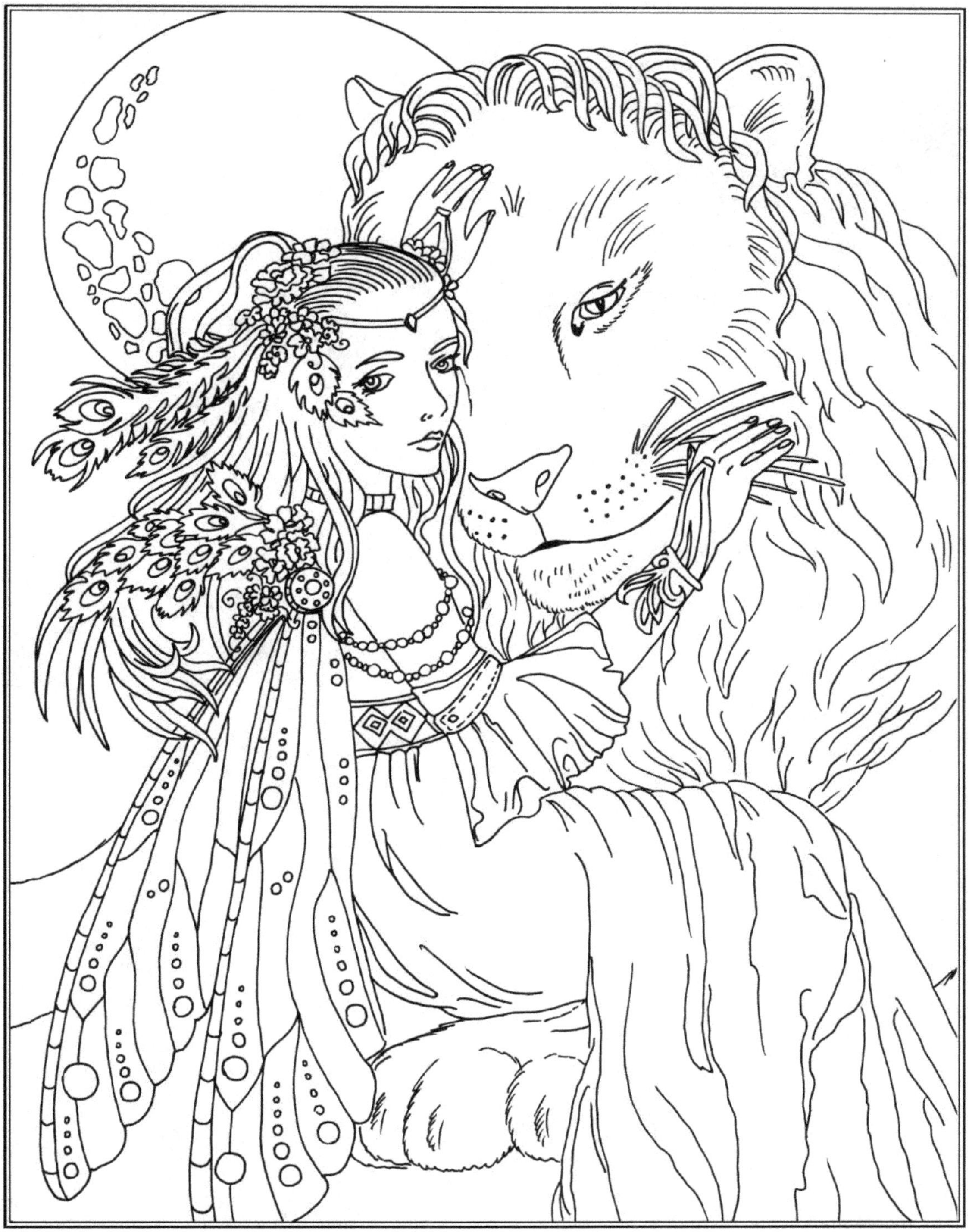

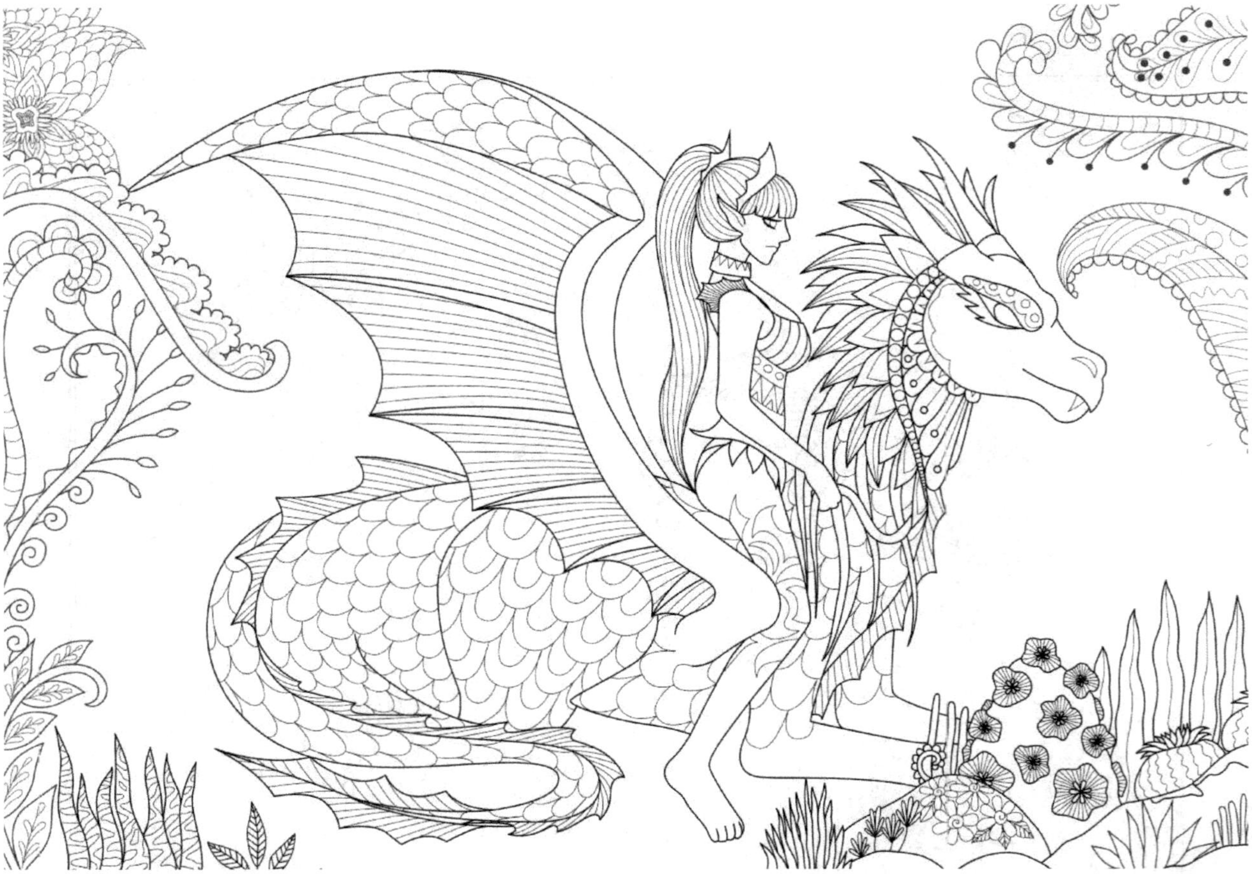

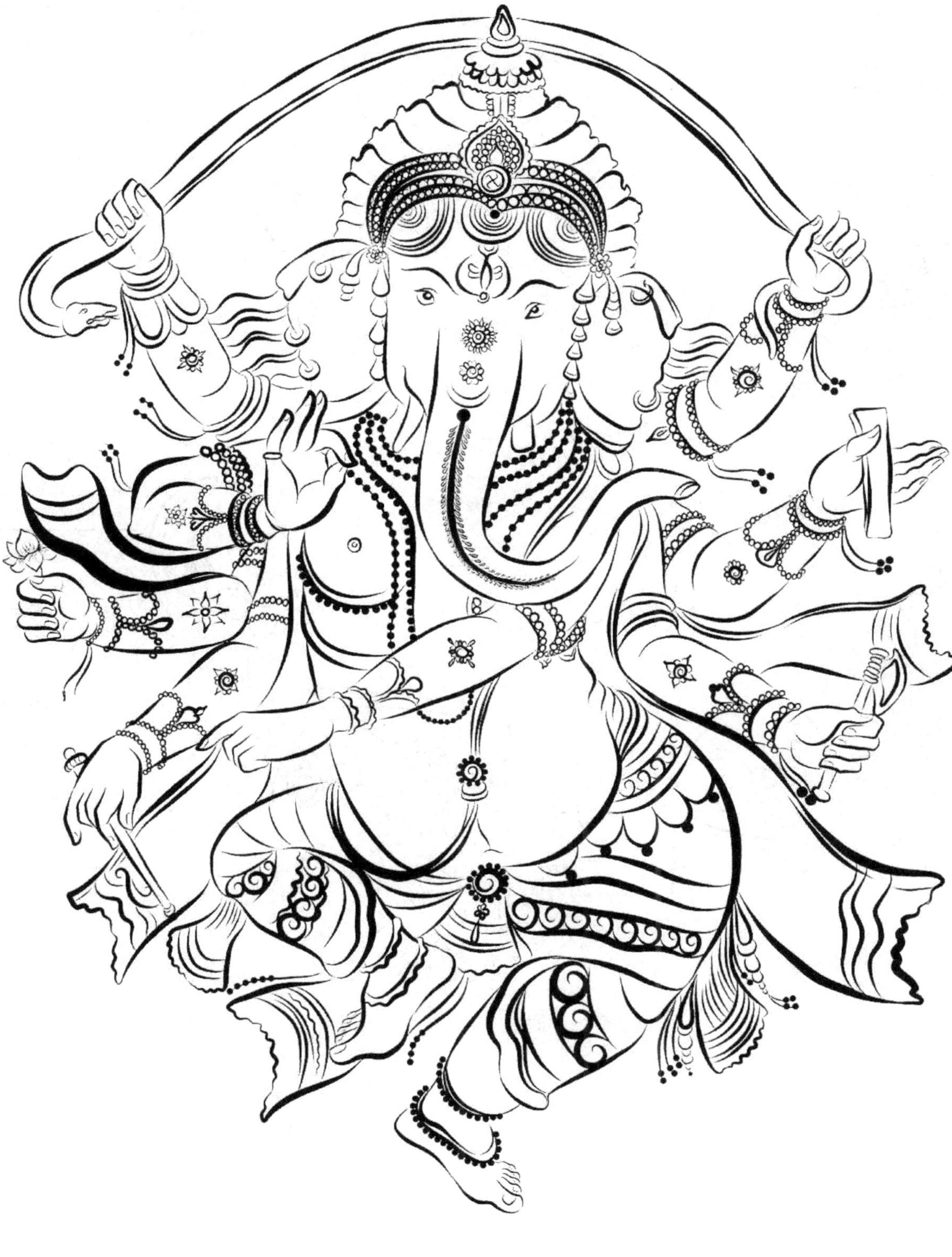

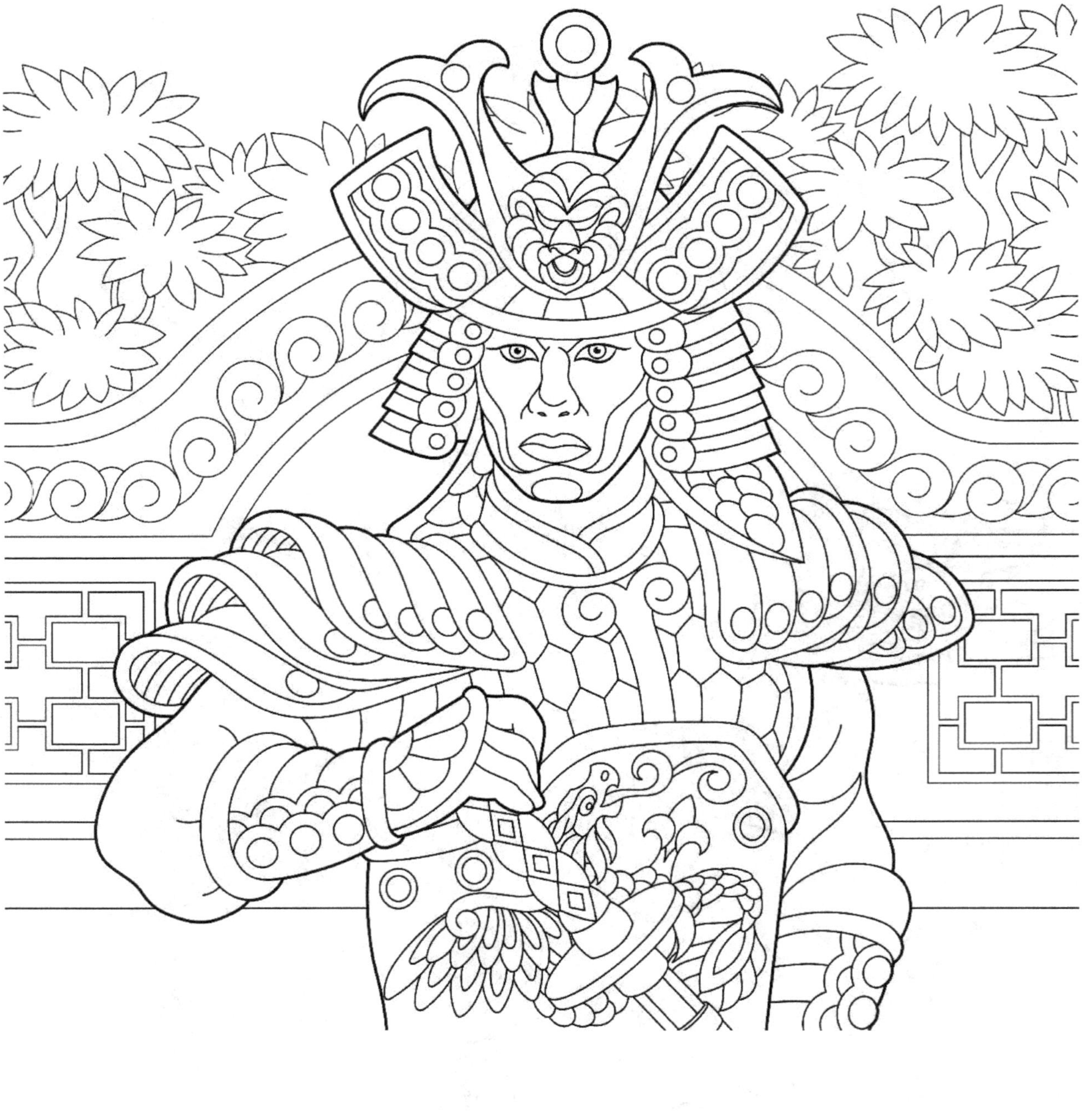

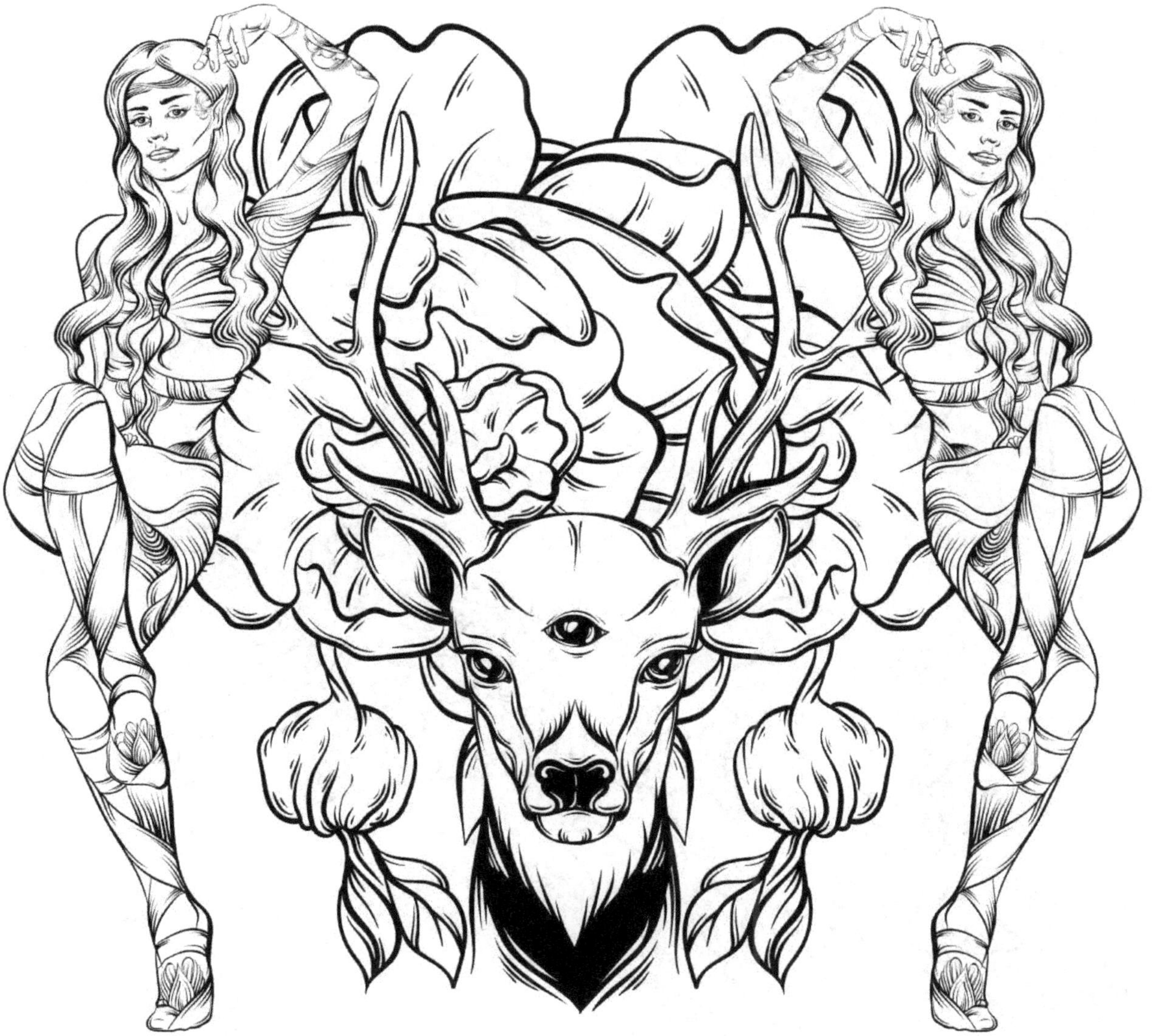

Gemini

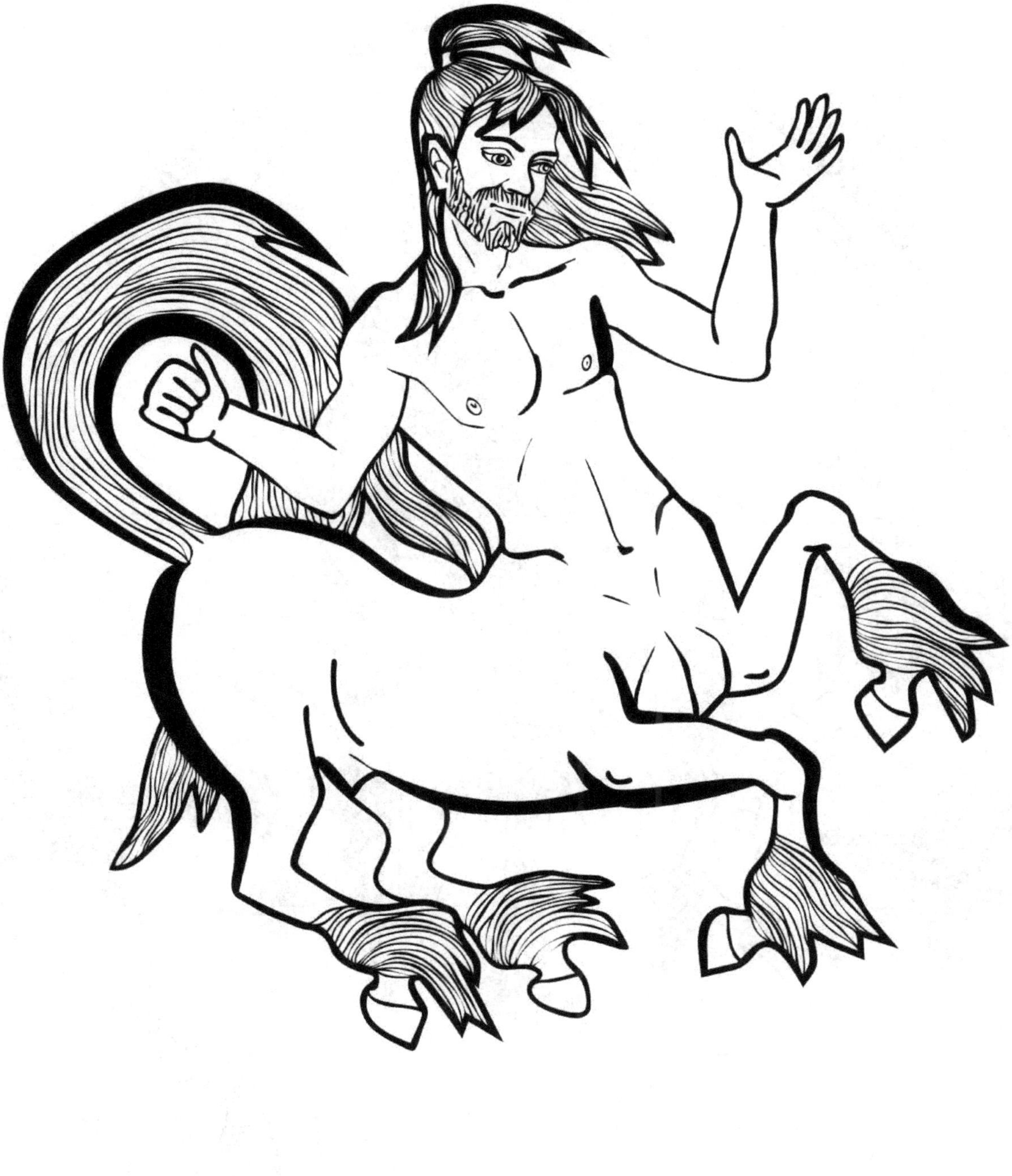

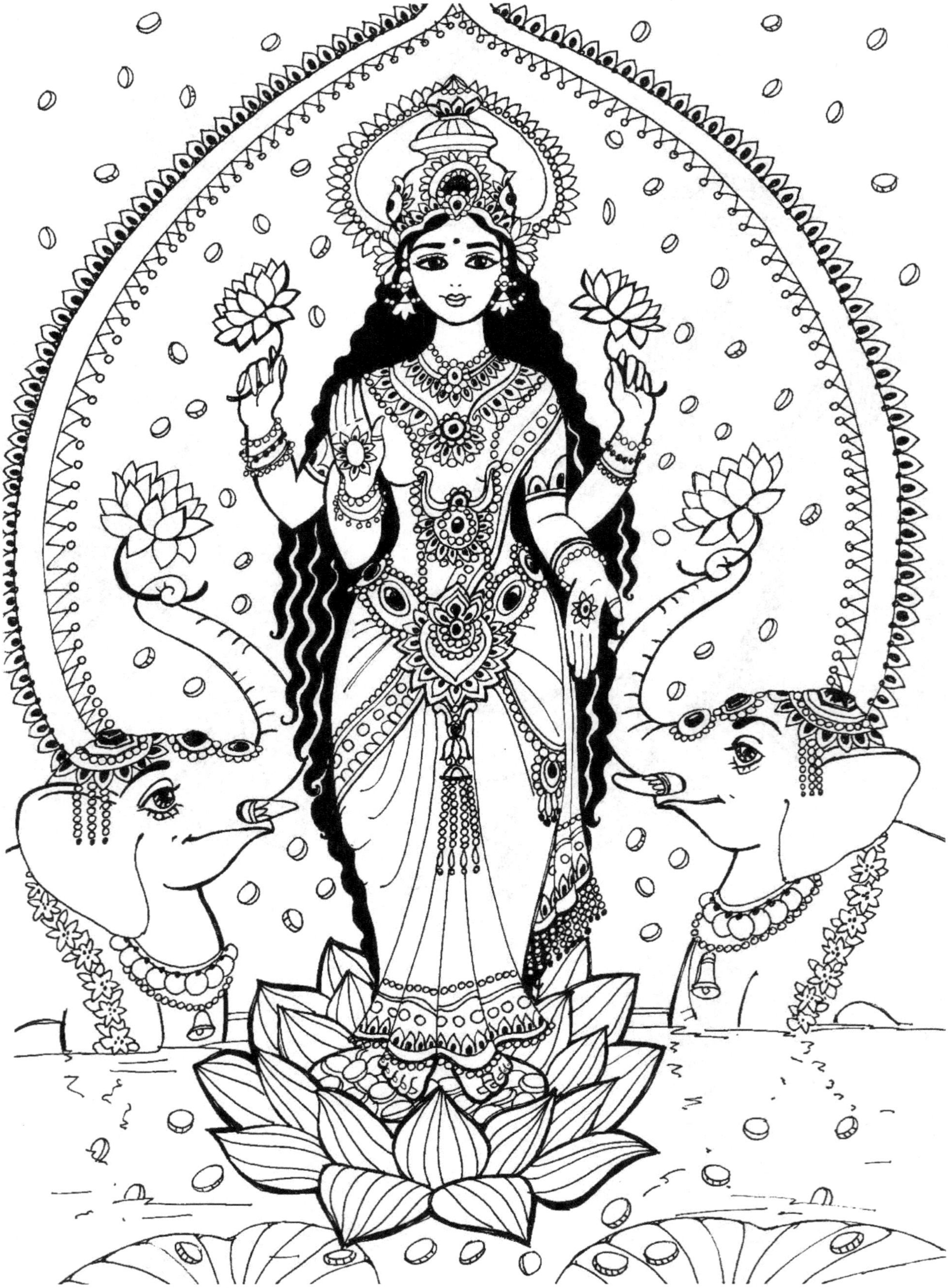

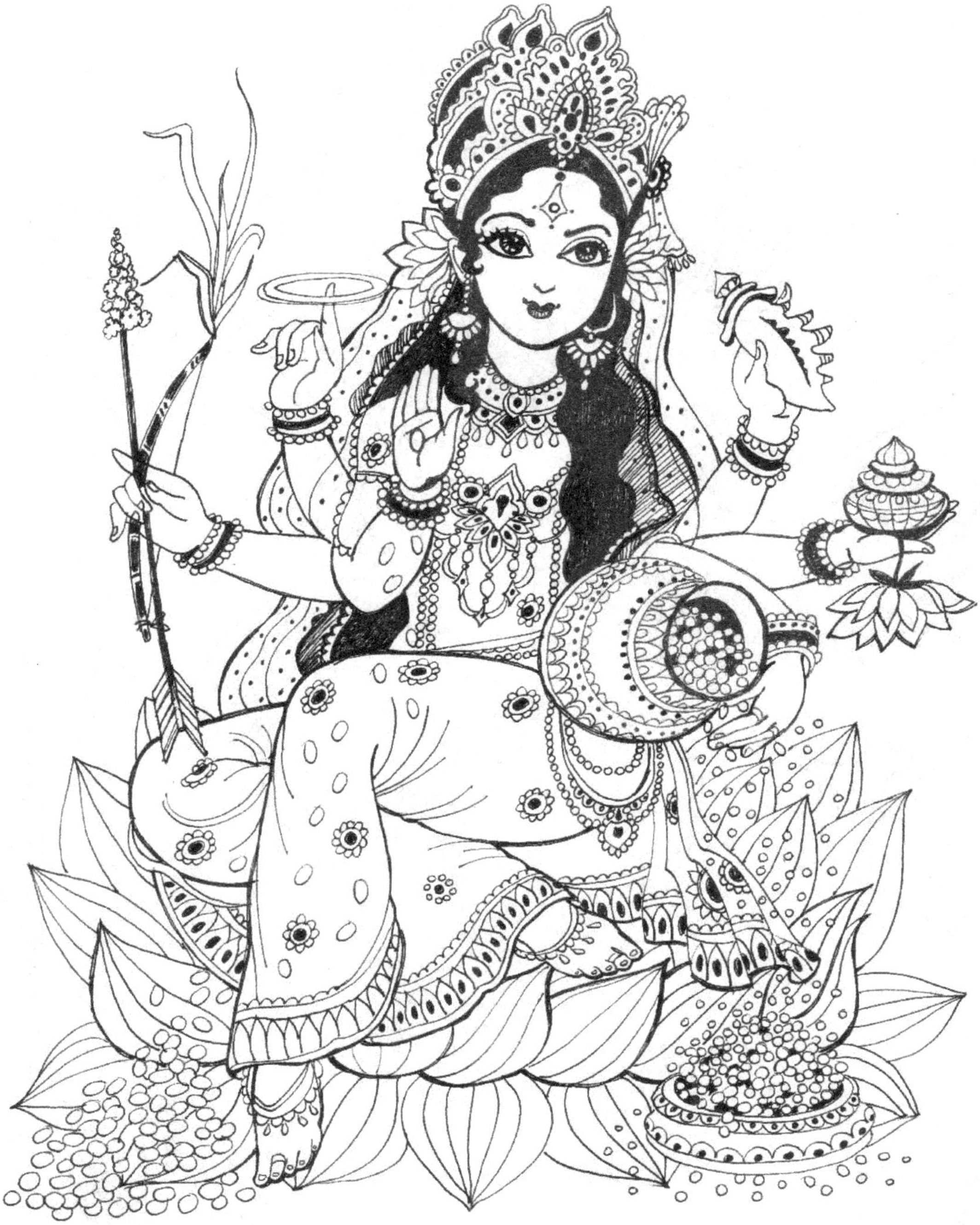

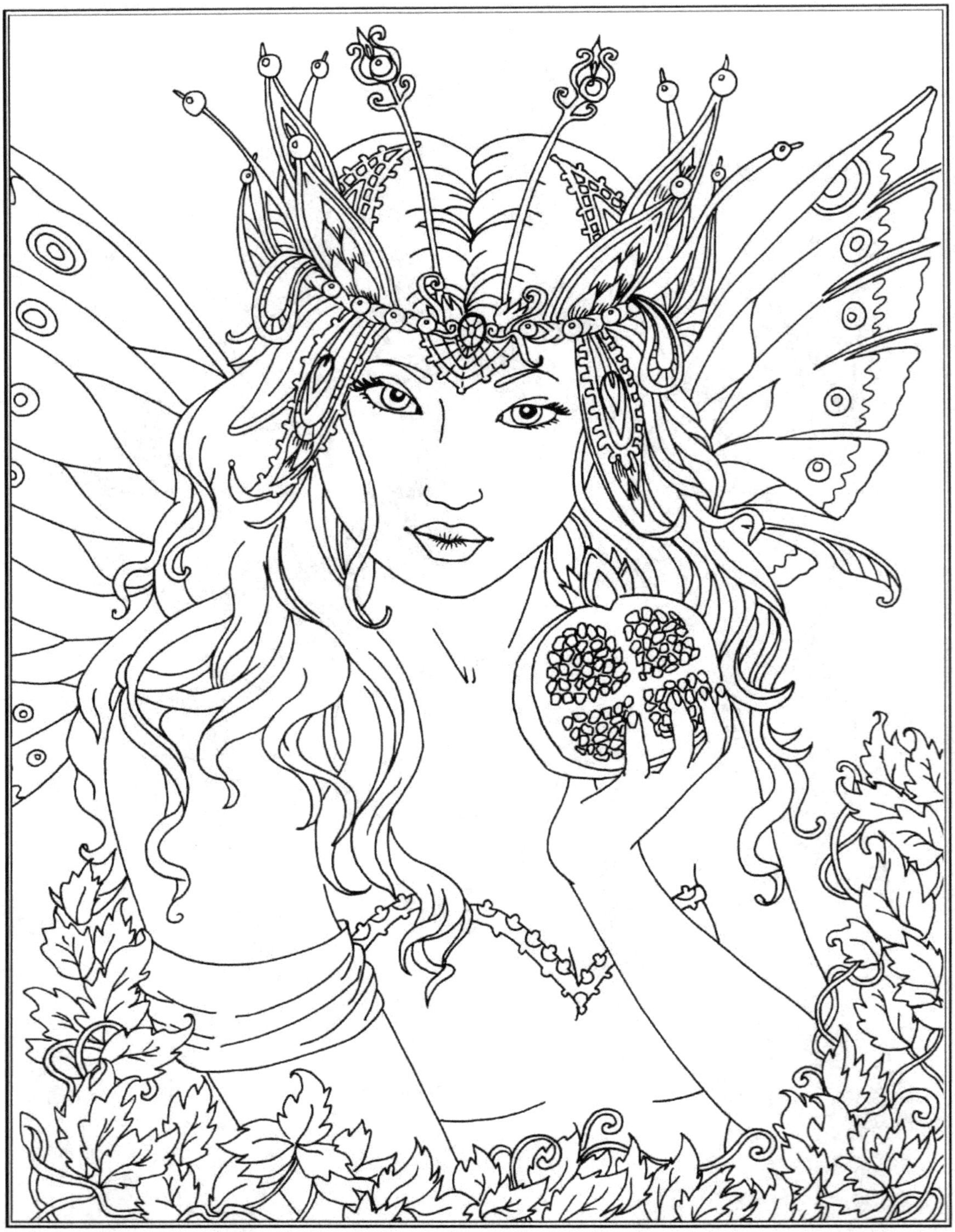

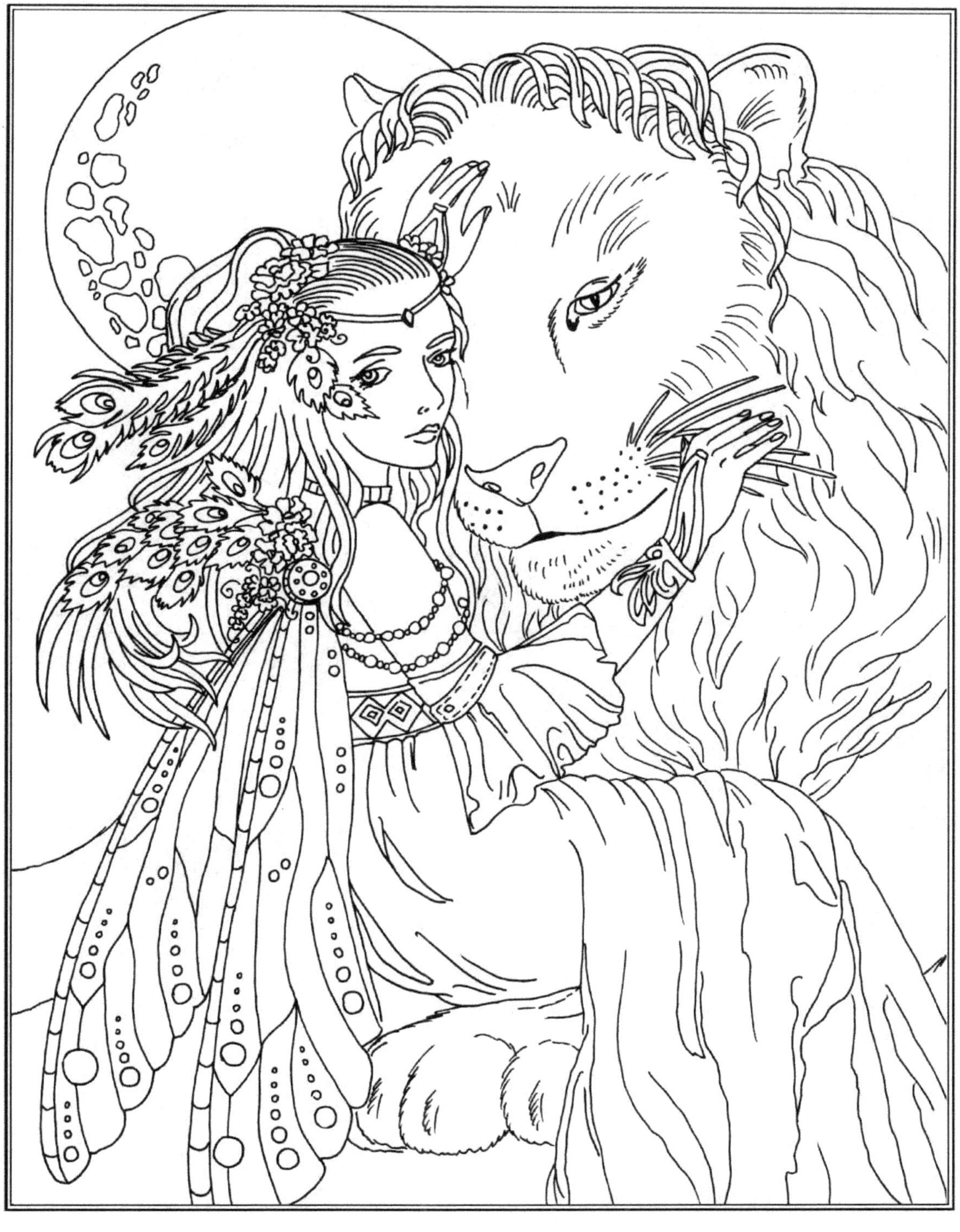

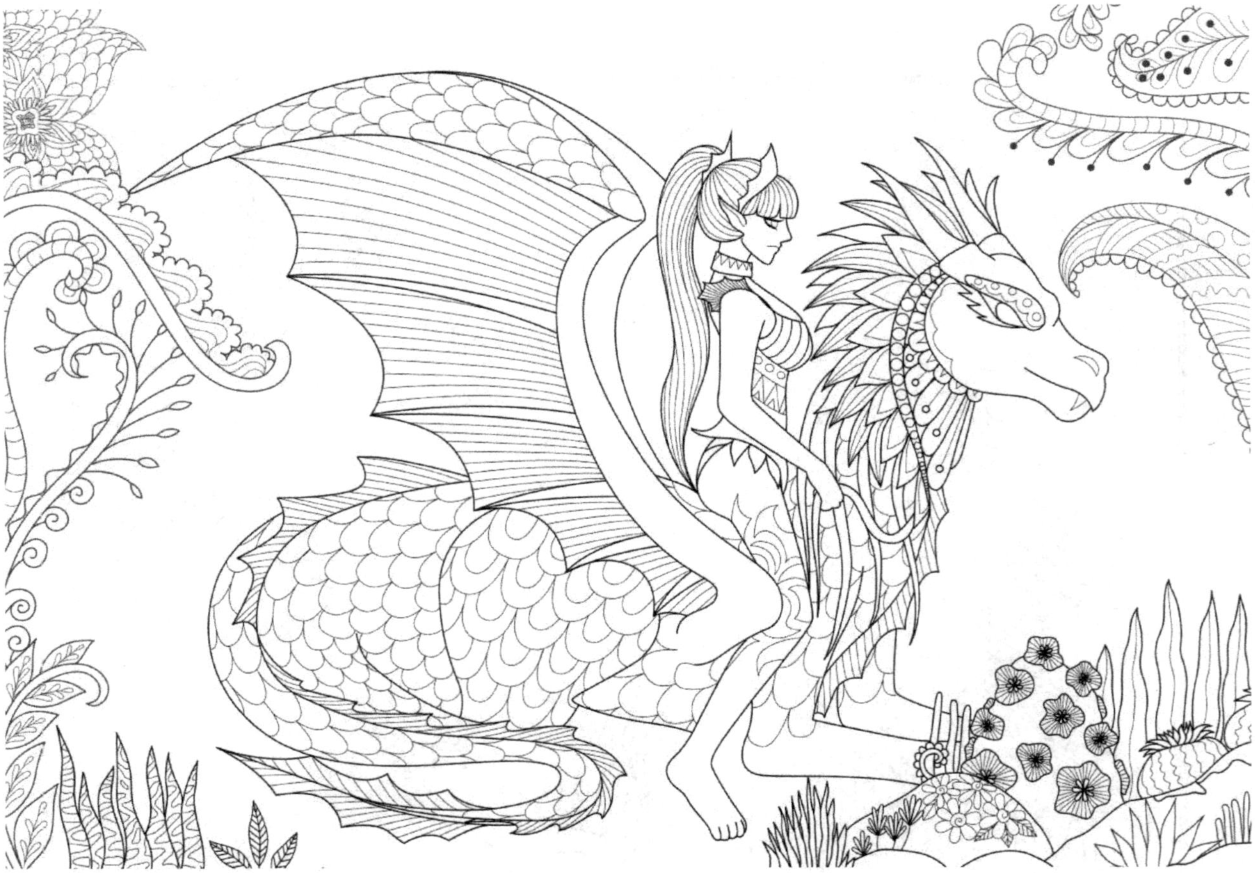

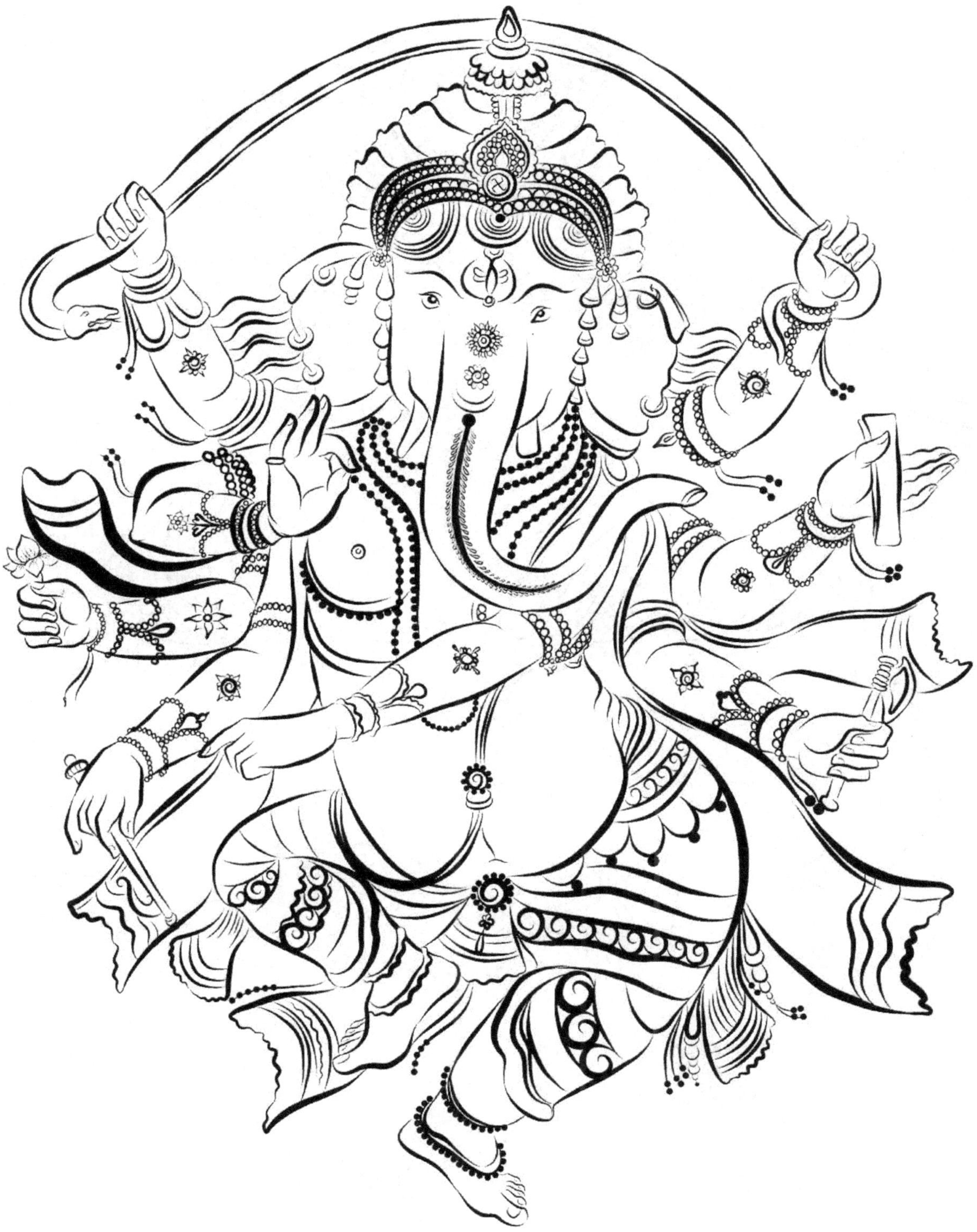

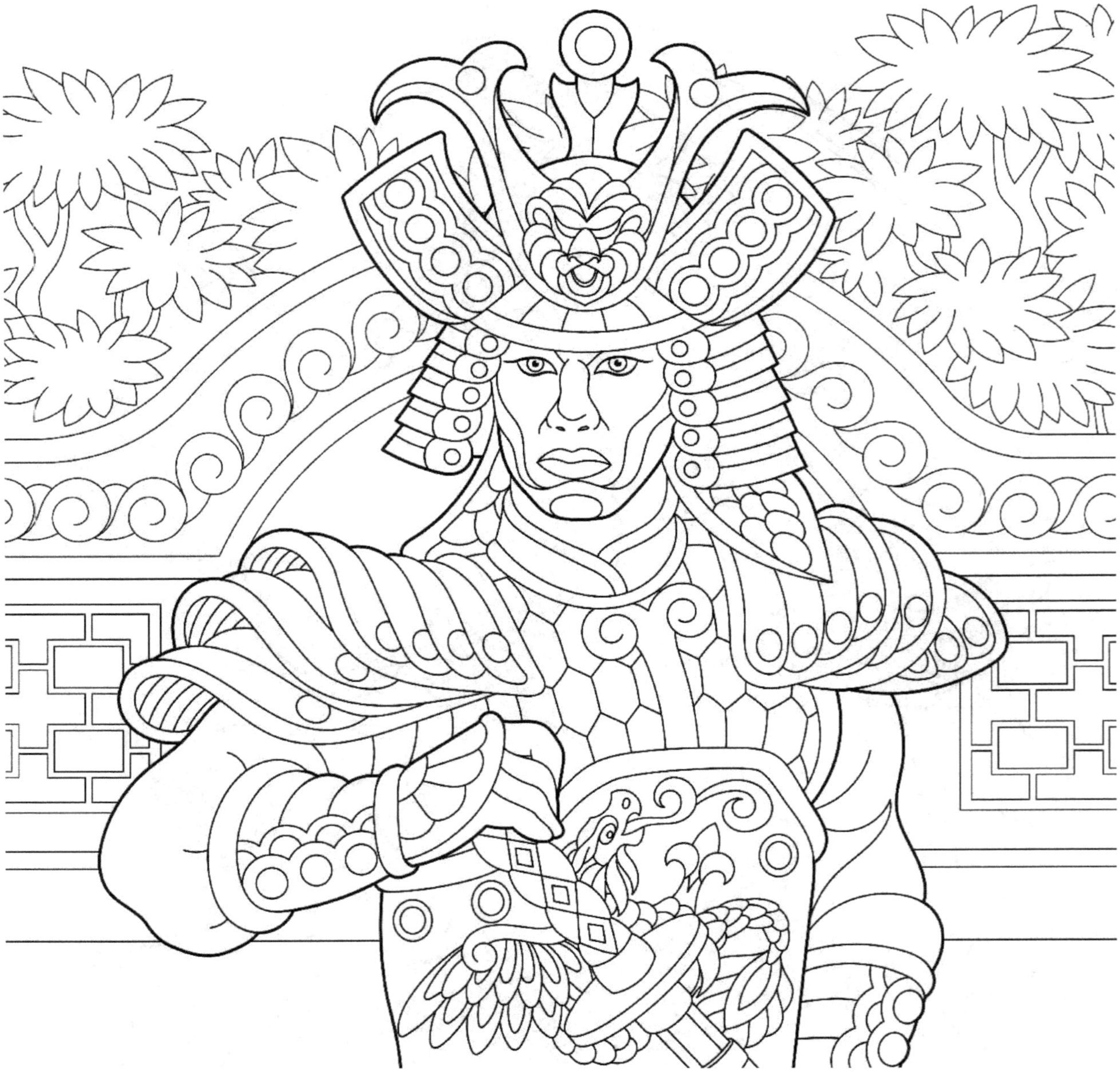

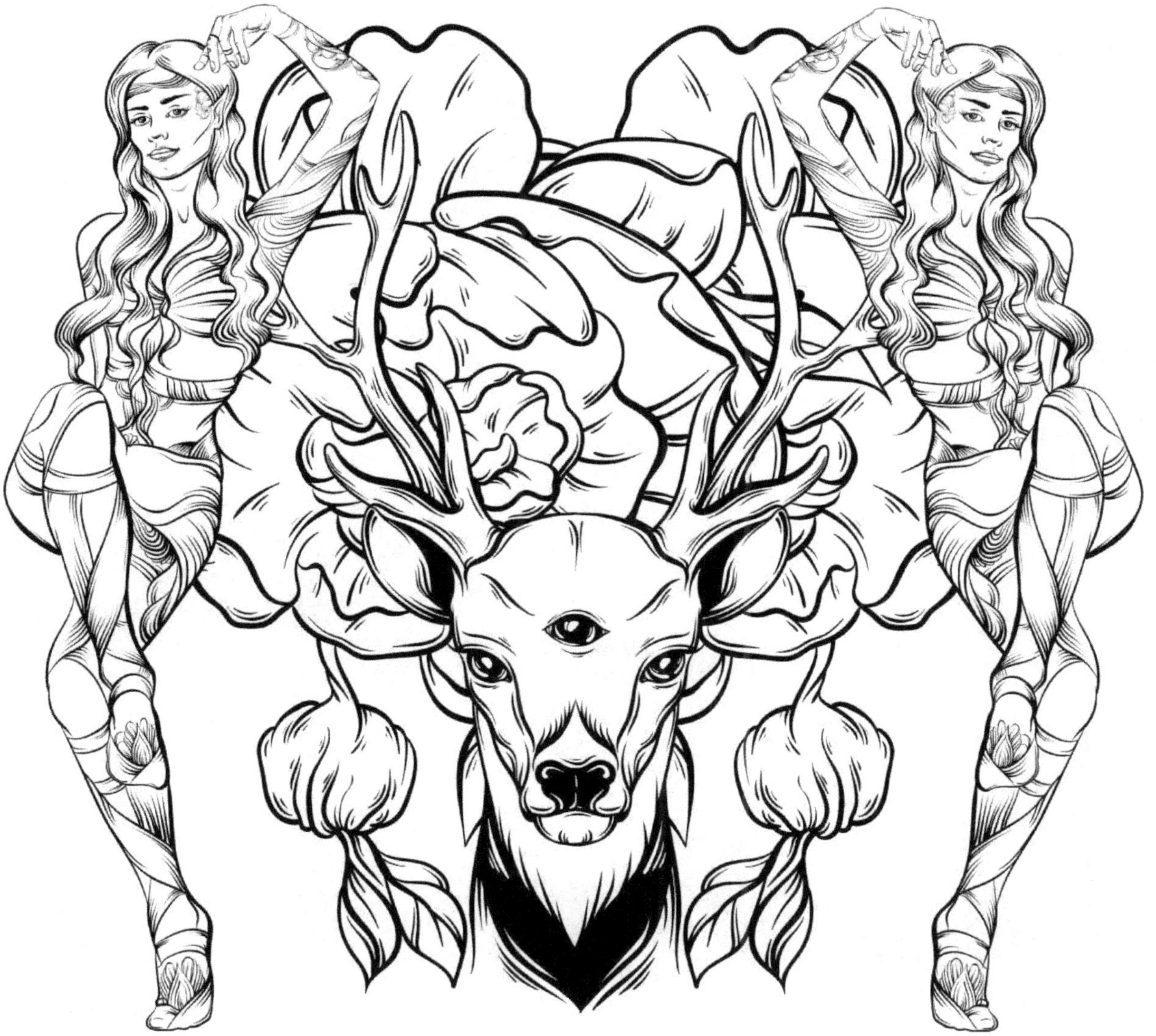